TEXT, TITLE, and
JACKET HANDLETTERED
BY OHARA HALE

enchantedlionbooks.com

First American edition published in 2015 by Enchanted Lion Books,
351 Van Brunt Street, Brooklyn, NY 11231
Translated from the French by Claudia Zoe Bedrick
Copyright © 2015 by Enchanted Lion Books for the English-language translation
Originally published in France in 2014 as *Louis Ier, Roi des moutons*
Copyright © 2014 by Actes Sud
All rights reserved under International and Pan-American Copyright Conventions
A CIP record is on file with the Library of Congress
ISBN 978-1-59270-185-8
Printed in Italy by Grafiche AZ

First Printing

LOUIS I
KING OF the SHEEP

OLIVIER TALLEC

ENCHANTED LION BOOKS
NEW YORK

AND SO IT WAS ONE WINDY DAY THAT LOUIS the SHEEP THEREBY BECAME LOUIS I, KING OF the SHEEP.

THE FIRST THING LOUIS I THOUGHT WAS THAT
TO GOVERN, A KING SHOULD HAVE A SCEPTER.

AND A THRONE FROM WHICH TO HAND DOWN
JUSTICE, BECAUSE JUSTICE IS RATHER IMPORTANT.

AND A GRAND KING'S BED WHERE ALL COULD
BEHOLD HIM AS HE SETTLED DOWN FOR the NIGHT.

LOUIS I ALSO TOLD HIMSELF THAT A GOOD KING
SHOULD ADDRESS HIS PEOPLE FROM TIME TO TIME.

OTHER THAN THAT, HE WOULD SPEND HIS TIME HUNTING, CHASING AFTER DEER, WILD BOARS and, ABOVE ALL, LIONS.

BUT SINCE THERE WERE NO LIONS IN HIS KINGDOM, HE WOULD HAVE THEM BROUGHT TO HIM FOR HIS PLEASURE.

HE'D ALSO STROLL THROUGH HIS ROYAL GARDENS,
WHICH WOULD BE TENDED BY ONLY the BEST GARDENERS.

And LOUIS I WOULD RECEIVE the WORLD'S GREATEST ARTISTS AT HIS PALACE, WHERE THEY WOULD PERFORM BEFORE HIM and HIS COURT.

AMBASSADORS FROM FAR and WIDE WOULD ALSO TRAVEL
LONG DISTANCES TO PAY TRIBUTE TO HIM, KING OF the SHEEP.

BUT FIRST and FOREMOST, LOUIS I DECIDED,
HE MUST BRING ORDER TO HIS KINGDOM.

SO HE COMMANDED HIS PEOPLE TO
MARCH BEHIND HIM IN SHEEP STEP.

NEXT, LOUIS I DECIDED THAT ONLY the SHEEP
WHO RESEMBLED HIM COULD LIVE AT HIS SIDE.

The OTHERS MUST BE DRIVEN OUT.

BUT THEN, UPON ANOTHER WINDY DAY...

LOUIS I, KING OF the SHEEP, BECAME
LOUIS the SHEEP ONCE AGAIN.